NIC BISHOP
MARSUPIALS

scholastic 💡 nonfiction

an imprint of

📖 SCHOLASTIC

To Vivien,

who joined me on many

marsupial expeditions

For their kind help, the author would like to thank
Amber Yarde, Kanyana Wildlife Rehabilitation
Centre, Lions Dryandra Village, Lisa Dabek,
Perth Zoo, Trowunna Wildlife Park, and
Wildlife Wonderland.

LIBRARY OF CONGRESS CATALOGING-IN-PUBLICATION DATA
Bishop, Nic, 1955– • Nic Bishop marsupials. • p. cm.
1. Marsupials—Juvenile literature. I. Title.
II. Title: Marsupials.
QL737.M3B57 2009 • 599.2—dc22

ISBN-13: 978-0-439-87758-9 • ISBN-10: 0-439-87758-X
10 9 8 7 6 5 4 3 2 1   09 10 11 12 13

Printed in Singapore 46
First printing, September 2009
Book design by Nancy Sabato

*This brushtail possum has
large eyes to see at night.
The marsupial on the title
page is a bettong in mid-hop.*

This baby kangaroo peeks out from the safety of its mother's pouch. A mother kangaroo regularly bathes her baby and cleans her pouch by licking them.

Most people know about lions, zebras, monkeys, and bears, but what about bettongs and bilbies? Or potoroos and pademelons? Dibblers and dunnarts?

These animals live on the continent of Australia, along with kangaroos, koalas, wombats, and a whole crew of amazing creatures. And it's not only their names that are neat. Each mother raises her babies inside a furry pouch, or pocket, on her belly. This special pouch is called a *marsupium*, and these animals are called marsupials.

Marsupials are mammals, like cats, dogs, horses, and humans.

All mammals have hair, or fur. They also have warm blood and raise their young on milk. But marsupials do one thing very differently. They give birth to babies that are so small, they look like pink jelly beans with two little legs. Some marsupial babies are tinier than a grain of rice.

Such a baby is far too little and undeveloped to look after itself. So as soon as it is born, it must wriggle and climb through its mother's fur until it reaches the warm safety of her pouch. Then it crawls inside to take a nipple in its mouth and doesn't let go. It feeds and grows on its mother's milk for weeks or months until it is big enough to leave the pouch and start caring for itself.

The boodie is the size of a rabbit and lives in Australia's desert. It stays cool by resting in burrows that it digs. It hops out at night to nibble grasses, roots, seeds, and fungi.

Not all marsupials live in Australia. There may be one very much at home in your backyard. **The Virginia opossum is the only marsupial found in the United States, and it's tough.** Long ago, its ancestors lived in the warm, tropical forests of Central America. Now it has spread as far north as Canada, where it survives the iciest winters.

The Virginia opossum is *nocturnal*, meaning that it is active at night. It climbs trees with the help of a *prehensile tail*, which it wraps around branches for extra grip. The opossum's best-known trick is playing dead. When a *predator* scares it, the opossum suddenly keels over with its mouth open and its eyes glazed. It won't move a whisker, even if you tickle it. It can keep up this act for hours, until the confused predator wanders away.

The Virginia opossum eats almost anything, including insects, fruit, frogs, snails, and tasty treats from your garbage. It also likes eating snakes and can survive being bitten, even by a rattlesnake.

Another ninety or so types of opossums live in Central and South America. Many are secretive, and not much bigger than mice. They scamper and climb through the forest after dark. Few people ever notice them, so there are sure to be new kinds waiting to be discovered.

Most of these small opossums do not have pouches. Babies have to cling to their mother's belly instead, which can be tricky. They sometimes get bumped or even fall off, though a mother may go back to collect a wailing youngster. When they get bigger, the young sensibly climb on their mother's back.

One of the most unusual opossums is the yapok, or water opossum. It has webbed hind feet, like a beaver, to swim underwater. The yapok also has a waterproof pouch, so its young stay warm and dry while their mother dives for frogs, shrimp, and small fish.

The short-tailed opossum relies on its good sense of smell and long whiskers to find its way through the undergrowth at night. This one is sniffing my camera.

The absolute best places to see marsupials are Australia and the nearby island of New Guinea. There are more than 220 types of marsupials here, from boodies that dig burrows in the desert to possums that glide from tree to tree. There are even marsupial moles that spend their lives underground.

An eastern grey kangaroo, which stands five feet tall, can leap twenty-five feet in one bound and outrun a horse. It uses its long tail for balance as it hops.

Kangaroos are the most famous marsupials, known for their incredible hopping. They do this with the help of special stretchy tendons, like bungee cords, in their legs. These pull tight when the kangaroo lands and then twang back to help launch it on its next hop. It's a great way to go fast. A red kangaroo can hop twenty miles an hour with half as much effort as a dog trying to chase it. And if it wants, a red kangaroo can sprint away at forty miles an hour and leap over an eight-foot fence. Few animals can match that!

Kangaroos are also hardy. Red kangaroos live in Australia's incredibly hot, dry deserts. They survive on almost as little water as camels do. In fact, they can get all their water from the plants they eat, so they may not need to drink for weeks. Kangaroos also eat plants so tough that their chewing teeth, called *molars*, get ground away. Luckily, they grow new teeth as the old ones wear out.

In Australia, a baby marsupial is called a *joey*, and a kangaroo mother nearly always has one in her pocket. After one joey leaves her pouch, she licks it clean and makes it cozy for the next bean-sized baby to climb inside. Then she makes two very different types of milk. One kind is for her newborn. The other, which might be richer in fats, is perfect for the older joey outside the pouch. With such amazing adaptations, it's no wonder that kangaroos survive so well. They outnumber people in Australia.

A kangaroo mother sometimes play-fights with her joey. This is an important lesson for her young, which might need to fight other kangaroos as adults.

There are more than forty kinds of kangaroos in Australia.

The smaller ones are usually called wallabies, and they live in every environment. Hare wallabies can survive in deserts. Red-necked wallabies and their relatives, the pademelons, dwell in forests and emerge at dusk to feed in grassy glades.

The prettiest members of the kangaroo family are rock wallabies. They have soft fur that can be beautifully striped in colors of chocolate and cream. They are also amazing rock climbers. Their feet have large toe pads with rough patterns for gripping, like mountain bike tires. A rock wallaby moves as nimbly as an acrobat, twisting its long, graceful tail here and there for balance. It can skip along rocky ledges and bound straight up steep cliffs.

Like other kangaroos and wallabies, the red-necked wallaby tries to stay cool under the shade of a tree during the day. It comes out when the sun goes down or if it is cloudy.

Kangaroos, it seems, can live anywhere. Some even climb trees!

That's right! Early explorers didn't believe it either, when *indigenous* people told them that kangaroos lived in trees. It sounded as silly as fish living in sand dunes.

Eight of the ten types of tree kangaroos live in the misty forests of New Guinea. They are so secretive that you may search for years and never see one. But if you are very lucky, they are a wonderful sight. They have long, curved claws and strong arms for climbing. And their feet have large pads for gripping. Unlike all other kangaroos, which move both legs at once, tree kangaroos can walk by moving one leg at a time. This allows them to go backward, which is useful when a tree kangaroo finds itself at the end of a long, thin branch.

Matschie's tree kangaroo lives in the treetops of cloud forests, high in the mountains of New Guinea. It is one of the most elusive mammals in the world. Photographing one is a once-in-a-lifetime opportunity.

Bettongs and potoroos are some of the rarest hopping marsupials.

These tiny relatives of kangaroos are about the size of rabbits and quite shy. They bound through the undergrowth late at night, busily sniffing here and there for tasty fungi, insects, and tubers to eat.

Their sensitive noses are especially good at finding fungi called truffles, which grow underground. A rufous bettong may travel several miles each night, digging up these favorite treats with its front paws. Before sunrise, it will gather soft grasses for bedding and hop back to its nest, hidden in the undergrowth.

The rufous bettong doesn't wake up until at least an hour after the sun has set. It can use its long tail like an extra hand to carry twigs and grasses to its nest.

Nighttime is when most marsupials are up and about. As soon as the sun sets, you may be startled by a male koala, grunting and bellowing from the treetops. He is showing off to females and telling other males to stay away.

The koala's calls are surprisingly scary for an animal with cute, fluffy ears and button eyes. But then koalas are full of surprises. For instance, they eat the leaves of eucalyptus trees, which are so poisonous they would kill most animals.

Koalas deal with this by breaking down the poisons. They are also incredibly picky about which of the 600 or so types of eucalyptus they eat. Koalas even sniff each leaf before deciding if it is tasty and safe. Still, even the best eucalyptus leaves make a skimpy meal. Koalas get so little energy from what they eat that they have to take lots of naps. A koala sleeps about twenty hours every day.

The name koala is thought to come from an indigenous word meaning "no drink." The eucalyptus leaves that koalas eat contain enough water for them to live on, so they rarely need to come down to the ground to drink.

Another surprise is that a koala's pouch faces backward, toward its hind legs. It must be scary when the joey first peeks out at the ground below. Luckily the mother has special pouch muscles to make sure her baby stays safely inside. And there is one good thing about growing up in a back-to-front pouch. It makes it easy for the joey to lap up a special type of poop that the mother makes. This poop is called *pap*, and it is like green, mushy baby food. It helps the joey switch from drinking its mother's milk to eating leaves like a grown-up koala.

A joey first comes out of the pouch when it is about six months old, although it climbs back in if it is sleepy or scared. By the time it is twelve months old, the joey no longer drinks milk. It can now look after itself, but it lives near its mother for up to one more year.

An older koala joey usually rides piggyback while its mother climbs. But while she is sleeping, which is most of the time, the joey can get bored and hungry. This one is wondering when its mother will carry it off to find some leaves to eat.

The most amazing of all possums are those that glide from tree to tree.

They have flaps of skin between their front and back legs, which open like sails when they jump from a branch. The feathertail glider can glide up to 80 feet. That's a long way for an animal small enough to perch on your thumb. What's more, the feathertail glider has amazing sticky toe pads that allow it to run up smooth bark and even glass! The biggest glider is the greater glider. It can leap as far as 330 feet and looks like a large Frisbee floating over the treetops.

At night, sugar gliders leap from tree to tree in search of fruit, nectar, tree sap, and insects. They are very sociable and nest in groups of seven or so in tree holes.

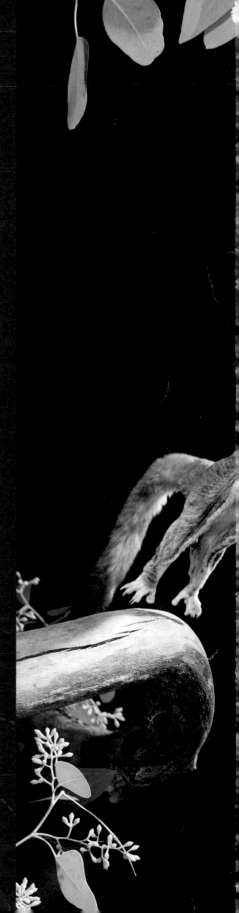

Brushtail possums may come to the ground to search for food at night. Possums were named by early explorers, who thought they looked like opossums from South America, but the two are not closely related.

Like koalas, possums live in trees and are good climbers. Possums' ankles twist more than any other mammal's, so their hind feet can face backward as they clamber down tree trunks headfirst. Most also have prehensile tails to curl around branches and hold on tight.

More than fifty types of possums live in Australia and New Guinea. Some, like the cuscus, have beautiful, fluffy fur. Others are interesting in different ways. The triok has black-and-white stripes like a skunk, and smells like one, too. The mountain pygmy possum lives like a mouse in snowy grasslands. It hibernates for months in the winter and lets its body temperature drop to near freezing. Then there is the noolbenger, or honey possum. This marsupial has a body barely longer than your little finger and a special feathery tongue. It runs from flower to flower, as busy as a hummingbird, lapping up almost its body weight in nectar every night.

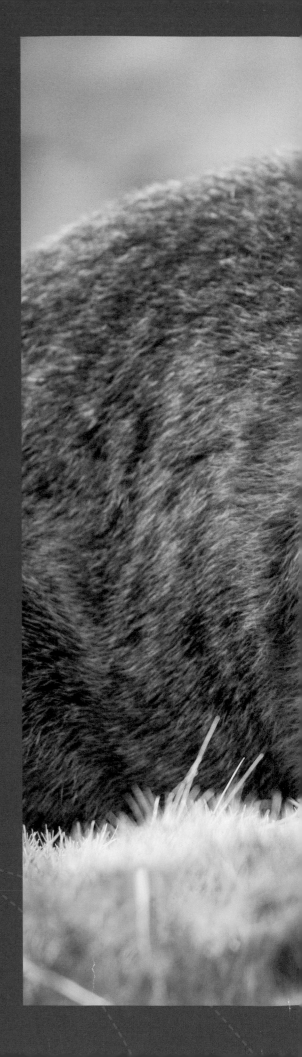

The wombat has a pouch that faces backward, just like the koala. However, this makes good sense for a wombat because it lives in a burrow. After all, what joey would want a face full of dirt?

A wombat will amble out of its burrow at sunset to nibble grasses and small plants. It may look slow and muddleheaded, but it has good senses of smell and hearing. **If it detects danger, a wombat can move its sixty-pound body as fast as an Olympic sprinter and dive into the nearest burrow.** Once inside, its big round bottom fits so snugly it can block the tunnel. Its rear end is protected with thick skin and super-bristly fur, like a shield to keep out intruders.

Wombats can live for more than fifteen years. They are probably the most intelligent marsupial and may be as smart as dogs. They are also known for being quite stubborn.

Wombats survive on very little. The hairy-nosed wombat thrives in desertlike conditions on a quarter of the food and water that most mammals need. Scientists are a bit puzzled about how it does this, although living in a burrow helps. Even if it is a scorching 105 degrees Fahrenheit outside, a wombat burrow will stay a comfy 78 degrees Fahrenheit. **To save energy, a wombat can also slow its heart rate and breathing while napping.** And it is so good at absorbing water from the leaves it eats that wombat poops are probably the driest of any mammal's.

A wombat burrow may be used for generations and can be as long as 100 feet, with tidy sleeping chambers carpeted in soft, dry grass. Usually just one animal lives in a burrow, and visitors are asked to leave, with lots of huffing and grumbling. Most wombats prefer their own company.

A wombat spends about three-quarters of its time in its burrow, often sleeping, and perhaps snoring too. You can see this baby wombat's large digging claws and tiny tail. Her two big toes lack claws so they can be used to wipe sensitive areas, like her eyes.

At first, the bilby looks like a mix-and-match puzzle.

It has the ears of a rabbit, the legs of a kangaroo, the body of an aardvark, and the silky soft fur of a chinchilla. But there is no question that it is suited to life in the desert.

The bilby has long claws to dig a burrow six feet deep, where it can stay cool during the day. It comes out at night to sniff for food with its long nose. Insects, lizards, seeds, and roots are some of its favorites. Meanwhile, its large ears listen for danger. And if it is frightened, it can bury itself under the sand in minutes.

A bilby moves on all four legs but often stands up on its back feet to check things out. To sleep, it folds its ears over its eyes and tucks its head between its front paws.

Australia's marsupial *carnivores* come in miniature. The long-tailed planigale is the smallest marsupial in the world, with a body just two inches long. Yet it is not short on ferocity. A planigale will attack a grasshopper as big as itself just as fearlessly as a lion attacks a zebra.

There are about fifty kinds of these mini meat-eaters, including dibblers, dunnarts, mulgaras, and ningauis. All are fast and agile. They have to be, since many need to eat about their body weight in food every night. Cockroaches, spiders, lizards, and even scorpions are not safe when these predators are on the prowl. After a night of hunting, they sleep under logs or in hollows. Sometimes, they curl up in groups to keep warm in cold weather.

The fat-tailed dunnart is no bigger than a mouse and makes a nest of grass, hidden under a log or in some rocks. It gets its name because it stores a day or two of food as fat in its tail.

As soon as the sun sets, a quoll will sneak into the night in search of *prey*. Large eyes and a good sense of smell help it hunt in the darkness. It prowls through the undergrowth, pouncing on lizards, snakes, insects, and other small marsupials. **Sometimes a quoll will climb trees, like a cat, to take possums, and birds and their eggs.** Occasionally, one may even tackle an animal larger than itself, such as a wallaby.

There are four types of quolls in Australia, but sadly all are rare. People have brought predators, such as cats and foxes, to Australia from other countries, and these animals compete with quolls for food. Luckily, they still thrive on the island of Tasmania, which is just south of the mainland of Australia.

The quoll is a carnivore the size of a cat, with a spotted coat like a little leopard. During the day, it sleeps inside a den, which may be in a hollow log or a burrow.

Tasmania is where the Tasmanian devil lives. These scrappy predators get especially excited by food, and they don't have good table manners. A devil can travel ten miles each night, hunting frogs, lizards, and small wallabies. But their favorite is something big that is already dead, like a kangaroo. And if it is starting to smell, then so much the better. A devil's nose will sniff such a meal from a mile away.

The Tasmanian devil was named by early settlers who were terrified by its bloodcurdling shrieks in the dead of night. But devils don't deserve their reputation. They are intelligent and playful in a mischievous way. These two are resting at their den.

A midnight feast is filled with squabbles and tugs-of-war over the best bits. **A Tasmanian devil can crunch through tough bones and thick skin.**

Its jaws are as powerful as those of a dog four times its size. It also eats fast, gulping almost half its weight in meat in just thirty minutes. Then it will be happy for a day or so, until it is thinking about food again.

A numbat does not have a pouch, so joeys cling to their mother's belly. When they are bigger, she leaves them in her den while she looks for termites.

Numbats are much more particular about what they eat. They only like termites and an occasional ant.

The numbat is one of the only marsupials that prefers to be busy during the day, when termites are out and about. It scampers across the forest floor, looking like a striped squirrel, and pokes its nose into every nook and cranny. If it sniffs termites, it slips out a sticky tongue about half as long as its body and laps them up. **A numbat can eat 20,000 crunchy termites a day.**

It is easy to marvel at marsupials. Gliding across treetops, hopping through grasslands, or burrowing beneath deserts, marsupials have found so many neat ways to survive.

I spent nearly six months in Australia while working on this book. It is a huge, hot, and often dry continent. Many times I found the heat unbearable, so I was amazed at how marsupials survived. But what impressed me most was their wonderfully trusting and inquisitive nature. I could not help falling in love with them.

My favorite moment was wandering among mobs of wild kangaroos just after sunset. Dozens of soft faces gazed at me in the evening light. Some stood so quietly that I wondered if I could pet them.

Another time I sneaked up to a wombat by wriggling on my belly for hours. I lay so close I could hear it breathing. But the wombat paid no attention to me. It was too busy munching grass. I waited for it to face my camera. And I waited. Then, just as the sun was setting, the wombat finally looked at me for a few seconds, eye to eye. It was as if it were granting me a precious moment to take my photograph.

Many other marsupials only come out late at night, when it is too dark to see. So I used a camera trap to photograph them. This device makes an invisible trigger beam of infrared light, which fires the camera shutter when an animal walks through it. First I put the trigger beam near a trail or some other place that the animal might come. Then I wired it to my camera and several flashguns. After that I left everything until the next morning. If I was really lucky, an animal would take its own photograph during the night.

Of course, things rarely worked out perfectly. Often I only got a photograph of a tail or a foot. One playful bettong thought my equipment was a jungle gym. It would leap on top of my camera. Then it discovered the wires I had carefully buried. It had hours of entertainment tugging them, until all my flash stands fell over.

I could never even be sure whether the right animal would turn up. Once I set up my camera to photograph a marsupial called a woylie. I put some peanut butter nearby to tempt it, but all I ever got were naughty brushtail possums. You can see them enjoying their midnight feast in this photograph.

One thing that made me sad was that some marsupials have become very rare. Early settlers brought predators to Australia, such as cats and foxes, which prey on those marsupials that are about the size of rabbits. Boodies, bilbies, and numbats have almost vanished. So I had to photograph some of these animals at wildlife parks, where people are breeding them. One day, when scientists have found a way to keep them safe, their young will be released back into the wild.

Index
Entries in **bold** indicate photographs.

Glossary

Carnivore An animal that eats meat.

Indigenous Relating to the original people who lived in a region or those who have lived there since earliest historical times.

Predator An animal that lives by hunting other animals for food.

Prehensile tail A tail that can seize or grasp something by wrapping around it.

Prey An animal that is hunted by another animal for food.